This edition published by Parragon in 2011

Parragon
Queen Street House
4 Queen Street
Bath BA1 1HE, UK

Copyright © 2011 Disney/Pixar

ISBN 978-1-4454-0968-9

Printed in China

DISNEY · PIXAR
FINDING NEMO

Adapted by Lisa Ann Marsoli
Illustrated by the Disney Storybook Artists
Designed by Disney's Global Design Group

Bath · New York · Singapore · Hong Kong · Cologne · Delhi
Melbourne · Amsterdam · Johannesburg · Auckland · Shenzhen

6

THE DROP-OFF

At the edge of the Great Barrier Reef in Australia, a brood of clownfish was getting ready to hatch. Marlin and Coral, the mother and father, proudly watched over their eggs in the grotto.

"We still have to name them," Coral said. "I like Nemo."

Suddenly, a barracuda appeared. Marlin rushed
to protect Coral, but the barracuda's tail knocked him
out cold.

Marlin awoke to an eerie silence. When he swam
to the grotto, he found only one tiny egg – injured
but still OK.

"There, there, there. It's okay. Daddy's here," Marlin said softly, cradling the egg in his fin. "I promise I will never let anything happen to you . . . Nemo," he whispered to the egg.

9

From that day on, Marlin was very
protective of his son - especially since
Nemo was born with a 'lucky' fin. It was
smaller than his other fin and made him
an awkward swimmer. When it
was time for Nemo to start
school, Marlin didn't want to let
his son go.

But Nemo couldn't wait!

"Dad, how old are sea turtles?"
Nemo asked on the way to school.

"Well, if I ever meet a sea turtle,
I'll ask him," Marlin said.

At school, Nemo climbed on the back
of the teacher, Mr. Ray.

To his horror, Marlin learned that Mr. Ray was taking the class on a trip to the Drop-off - the very cliff where Coral and the eggs had been attacked!

"Come on, Nemo!" Nemo's new friends sneaked away from the rest of the class. At the edge of the Drop-off, they dared each other to swim up and touch a boat anchored nearby. "How far can you go?" Tad, one of Nemo's classmates, said to the clownfish.

Just then, Marlin swam over. "Nemo! No!" he cried.

"Dad, I wasn't going to go..." Nemo said, starting to explain.

"You think you can do these things, but you just can't!" his father said angrily.

"I hate you," Nemo mumbled.

Mr. Ray heard the commotion and swam over to help. While Marlin was busy talking to the teacher, Nemo swam to the boat and touched it with his fin. He was tired of his dad thinking he was too little and too weak to do anything!

When Marlin heard Nemo's classmates
shouting, he looked out toward the boat.
"Nemo!" he cried as a diver swam up right
behind his son.

"Swim, Nemo, swim!" the kids called.

"Daddy! Help me!" Nemo cried as the diver
scooped him up.

But before Marlin could do anything,
the diver-and Nemo-was already on the
boat. There was no way Marlin could catch up!

Marlin swam to a busy underwater passage. "Has anybody seen a boat? They took my son!" he cried.

Finally, a regal blue tang fish named Dory told him she had seen a boat. "Follow me!" she said.

But Dory had a problem: she couldn't remember anything for more than a few minutes. When she turned and saw Marlin, she got angry with him. "Stop following me, okay?" she exclaimed.

Suddenly, a big shark named Bruce showed up.

17

Bruce took Dory and Marlin to a sunken submarine. Inside was a meeting of sharks who claimed to be vegetarians. Marlin didn't trust them.

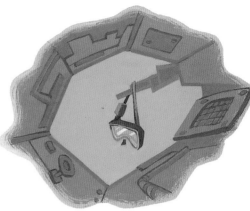

But then Marlin spotted a diving mask. It was just like the one worn by the diver who had captured Nemo! "What do these markings mean?" he wondered aloud. "I don't read human."

Suddenly, Bruce was overcome with hunger. He chased Dory and Marlin through the submarine, snapping his jaws. The pair raced into a tube that held a torpedo.

Marlin and Dory lodged the torpedo in Bruce's mouth to escape. The shark spat it out, and seconds later, it exploded!

MEET THE TANK GANG

Far away, a giant hand dropped
Nemo into unfamiliar waters.
Several friendly but strange fish
surrounded him. Bubbles, Peach,
Jacques, Bloat, Deb, and Gurgle
introduced themselves. Nemo was in a fish
tank in a dentist's office! The other fish were
thrilled to meet Nemo – a fish from the open sea!

Nigel, a pelican, flew to the window to say hello
to his tank friends. The dentist, Dr. Sherman, shooed
him away, knocking over a framed picture. Then Nemo
learned his fate: the little clownfish was going to be
given to Darla, Dr. Sherman's bratty niece . . . who had
shaken her last fish to death!

Then Nemo met the leader of the tank, Gill. Nemo noticed that Gill had a damaged fin, too, and felt a special bond with his new friend.

That night, the tank fish held a ceremony to accept Nemo into their group.

Gill nicknamed Nemo Shark Bait and shared his plan for how they would all escape from the tank — a plan that depended on little Nemo!

23

Meanwhile, Marlin woke after the torpedo's explosion. He and Dory were right on the edge of a deep trench. To make matters worse, Dory accidentally dropped the diver's mask!

As they swam down after the mask to darker waters, a glowing orb appeared. It was attached to a hungry anglerfish! While Marlin struggled with the fierce angler, Dory used the fish's light to see the writing on the mask.

"P. Sherman, 42 Wallaby Way, Sydney," she read.

After they escaped from the angler, Dory asked a school of moonfish to give her directions to Sydney. Marlin had already started swimming away when one of the moonfish gave Dory a tip. "When you come to a trench, swim *through* it, not *over* it," he warned her.

Soon Marlin and Dory reached the trench. But instead of swimming through it as Dory had suggested, Marlin convinced her to swim over it. They were instantly surrounded by a forest of jellyfish. How would they ever escape?

"All right. Here's the game!" Marlin cried. "Whoever can hop the fastest out of these jellyfish wins. You can't touch the tentacles — only the tops."

Dory had almost made it through when she got stung. Marlin pulled her free, but not before he was stung, too.

Back in the fish tank, Gill gave Nemo swimming lessons while the two swapped stories.

Gill caught Nemo looking at his biggest scar. "My first escape," Gill told him. "I landed on dental tools. I was aiming for the toilet. All drains lead to the ocean, kid."

Later, the fish began the first step of their escape plan: get the tank dirty. If they could break the filter, Dr. Sherman would have to clean the tank – and that would mean removing the fish and putting them in plastic bags. While the bags were on the counter, the fish would roll themselves out the window to freedom.

Coached by Gill, Nemo swam into the filter and wedged a pebble in the rotating fan.

But the pebble came loose and Nemo
was sucked toward the sharp blades.

The other fish rescued him, but Nemo
was terrified. The escape plan was ruined
and Gill realised he had put Nemo
in danger.

KEEP SWIMMING

Meanwhile, some sea turtles had rescued Marlin and Dory after their dangerous encounter with the jellyfish. "Takin' on the jellies — awesome!" Crush, a surfer turtle, proclaimed.

Marlin told the younger turtles the story of his quest to find his son. Soon the tale was being passed throughout the ocean from sea creature to sea creature, until Nigel overheard the news from

34 another pelican.

Nigel rushed back to the dentist's office
to tell Nemo that Marlin was on his way.
Inspired by his father's bravery, Nemo
grabbed a pebble and rushed over to the filter.
He successfully jammed it into the fan.
"Shark Bait, you did it!" the tank gang cheered.
They had two days until Dr. Sherman's niece
arrived. Now that the filter was broken, would the tank
get dirty enough to need a cleaning by then?

Out in the ocean,
Marlin and Dory bid the sea
turtles good-bye. Marlin called,
"Crush! How old are you?"
He couldn't wait to tell Nemo
the answer when he saw him.

Marlin and Dory swam and swam until they were lost. Dory asked a blue whale for directions, but they were sucked into its humungous mouth.

Just when it looked like things couldn't get any worse, the water inside the whale's mouth began to drain into its stomach!

Back in the tank, Nemo and his friends felt their luck was changing for the better. Without a working filter, the tank was a nice, slimy green.

Dr. Sherman swiped his finger across the inside of the glass. "Crikey!" he said with disgust. "I'd better clean the fish tank before Darla gets here."

The tank gang rejoiced.

"Are you ready to see your dad, kid?" Gill asked Nemo.

"Uh-huh!" Nemo cried happily.

41

42

The next morning when the fish woke up, the water was perfectly clear. The tank had already been cleaned by a brand-new, high-tech filter called the Aqua Scum 2003! The dentist would never have to clean the tank again.

"Boss must have installed it last night while we were sleeping," guessed Gill. The fish realized that their escape plan was ruined again.

"Wh—what are we gonna do?" Nemo asked, panicking.

Not far away, in Sydney Harbour, a blue whale surfaced and spouted. Riding atop the spray were Marlin and Dory!

"Dory! We made it!" Marlin cried joyfully. "We're going to find my son! All we have to do is find the boat that took him." The problem was, there were boats as far as the eye could see. Suddenly, a pelican swooped down and scooped them up.

The pelican landed on the dock, threw its head back, and prepared to enjoy its catch. "I didn't come this far to be breakfast!" Marlin cried. He and Dory stubbornly wedged themselves sideways in the bird's throat.

Nigel, perched nearby, watched as the choking
pelican stumbled around the dock. Nigel raced over and
whacked him on the back. Marlin and Dory flew out of
the pelican's mouth.

As he flopped helplessly on the dock, Marlin said with
a gasp, "I've got to find my son, Nemo!"

Nigel couldn't believe it. "He's that fish that's been fighting the whole ocean!" he exclaimed.

By this time, a flock of hungry seagulls had gathered. "Mine! Mine! Mine!" they shouted.

"Hop inside my mouth if you

want to live," whispered Nigel.

Marlin and Dory jumped inside Nigel's beak, and they were off. The seagulls followed, but Nigel's tricky maneuvers led the birds smack into a boat's sail.

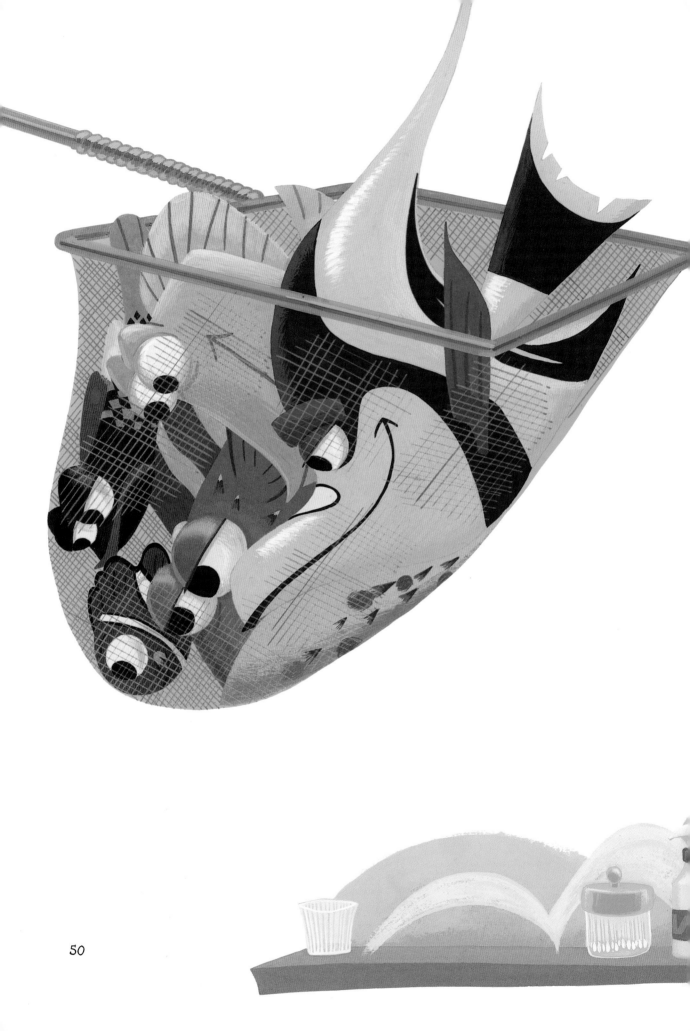

THE GREAT ESCAPE

Back at the dentist's office, Dr. Sherman stuck a net into the tank and captured Nemo. "Jump in and swim down!" Gill yelled. The rest of the tank gang joined Nemo in the net and forced it away from the dentist.

But suddenly, Dr. Sherman scooped Nemo into a plastic bag. Then he set the plastic bag by the tank.

"Roll, kid, roll!" the others cried. Nemo swam furiously back and forth. But the dentist spotted the wobbly bag and stuck it in a tray to keep Nemo from falling. Nemo and his friends were worried. Darla would be arriving any minute!

Suddenly, a bell rang!
Darla burst into the
room. "Fishy! Fishy!
Fishy!" the dentist's
niece cried.

Dr. Sherman reached
for the bag. Inside, Nemo was
floating upside down-playing dead!
Everyone in the tank cheered. If the dentist
flushed Nemo down the toilet, he'd travel through the
plumbing to freedom! But their joy instantly turned to
horror when Dr. Sherman started walking Nemo over
to the trash can instead!

Just then, Nigel showed up on the window ledge
and flew inside. The dentist dropped Nemo's bag onto
a sharp dental tool. The bag began to leak. Nemo
spotted Darla and played dead.

Marlin peeked out of Nigel's mouth and saw Nemo
floating upside down. He feared the worst.

Dr. Sherman pushed Nigel back outside and shut
the window.

Darla picked up Nemo's bag and shook it. Gill knew
he had to do something. The other tank fish launched
Gill out of the aquarium, and he landed right on
Darla's forehead!

Nemo fell out of the hole in the bag and onto a dental mirror on the tray. Gill flipped himself from Darla's forehead onto the tray. "Tell your dad I said hi," he said. Then he smacked his tail on the dental mirror, causing Nemo to fly over Darla's head and into the spit sink. Nemo escaped down the drain!

Back in the harbour, Nigel dropped
Marlin and Dory into the sea. Overcome
with sadness, Marlin said good-bye to
Dory. She pleaded to stay with him, as
he had become like family to her.
But it was no use.

Marlin couldn't stand to be around
any reminder of his failed search for his
son. He swam off and began his long
journey home.

55

Meanwhile, Nemo rode the rapids through the water treatment plant. When he finally poked his head out into daylight, he was greeted by two hungry crabs perched on the pipe. Nemo quickly swam away to avoid their snapping claws. He had just missed his dad passing by.

Escaping from the crabs, Nemo swam back toward the harbour and went off in search of his father. But instead, he found Dory swimming in circles and sobbing.

Dory and Nemo introduced themselves to each other – but of course Dory had no memory of Nemo or the search she had been on to find him. Nevertheless, the two swam off together.

Luckily, Dory spotted the word "Sydney" on the water treatment pipe. Suddenly, she remembered everything! She led Nemo back to where she had last seen Marlin.

Dory described Nemo's dad and asked the crabs if they had seen him. They wouldn't talk, until she threatened to turn them into seagull food!

"All right, I'll talk," one of the crabs cried. "He went to the fishing grounds!"

Dory and Nemo were reunited with
Marlin in the fishing grounds nearby. Before
they had a chance to celebrate, an enormous net
swept up Dory along with a huge school of groupers.

Thinking quickly, Nemo said, "Let's tell every fish
to swim down!"

Nemo swam inside the net to help. "Swim down!"
Marlin cried, and soon all the fish had broken through
the net. But where was Nemo?

Dory and Marlin found him beneath the net. Marlin
was relieved when Nemo's eyes fluttered open. "Dad, I'm
sorry. I don't hate you,"
Nemo said.

"Thank
goodness!"
Marlin cried.
"And guess
what? I met
a sea turtle.
They live to
be
a hundred and
fifty years old!"

Weeks later, Marlin and Nemo raced to school.
They had some amazing tales to tell – but most of
their friends didn't believe them. Then Bruce and
the other sharks showed up with Dory. Everyone's
mouths hung open as the giant sharks greeted
Marlin.

Nemo swam onto Mr. Ray's back, and the class started to leave. "Oh, wait! I forgot something," Nemo said.

Nemo swam back to his dad and gave him a big hug. "Love ya, Dad," said Nemo.

"I love you, too, son," said Marlin.

The End